# THE GOLDEN PRINCE

**Written by Tanuja Ramgolam**
*Illustrated by Frances Espanol*

To order additional copies of this book, contact:
Xlibris
UK TFN: 0800 0148620 (Toll Free inside the UK)
UK Local: 02036 956328 (+44 20 3695 6328 from outside the UK)
www.xlibrispublishing.co.uk
Orders@ Xlibrispublishing.co.uk

ISBN: 978-1-6641-1445-6 (sc)
ISBN: 978-1-6641-1446-3 (e)

Print information available on the last page

Rev. date: 02/05/2021

## <u>Dedication</u>

**This book is dedicated to my father Balroop Ramdin and my children.**

## <u>The Golden Prince</u>

Once lived a King and a Queen in a big palace. They did not have any children, that made the King and Queen sad.

The King's Minister came to see him. "There is a Sage in the village, people say he is very clever and he grant wishes" he informed the King "Why don't you talk to him, see if he can grant you the wish of having a child your Majesty."

"Go! Send the soldiers to bring him to me." ordered the King.

That afternoon the Sage came to the palace. The King told him about his worries of not having an heir to the throne.

The Sage asked the King "What will you give me in return?"

"Anything you desire." replied the King

"I will grant you the wish of two sons, but you will have to give me your first-born child." said the Sage.

"At least I will have one son with me for an heir even if I give him my first born." thought the King to himself. The King agreed. The Sage gave him an apple "Give this to your Queen, she must eat all of it even the seeds, she mustn't throw anything away. I will come back when your son turns eighteen." he left immediately.

After nine months the Queen gave birth to two boys. Everyone was happy. The King gave the people of his kingdom gifts and money. The princes were named James and Henry and they were brought up with love and affection. The King hired the best teachers to educate them. They were taught fencing, hunting and ballroom dancing.

Years passed; the princes grew into handsome young men. The day they turned eighteen the Sage came. The King was horrified to find the Sage at his front door. He had forgotten about his promise. The King pleaded with the Sage to spare his eldest son; he can have anything he wanted instead.

The Sage refused "You made a promise". The King rushed to tell Prince James all about the Sage. "Don't worry father I will keep your promise." Prince James bid good bye to the Queen and the King, his brother and everyone in the palace. He left with the Sage. The Queen was inconsolable, but she knew he was a strong brave man able to take care of himself.

On their way to the Sage's house, they came to a cross road. The Sage said to the Prince, "These two roads lead to my house, the road on the left is long, filled with flowers and butterflies, the road on the right is short, but there are monsters and ferocious animals in there, which one would you choose?" Without hesitation the Prince said the one on the right. He was pleased with the Prince's choice. He is brave thought the Sage.

Prince James took his sword out and went ahead, he fought the ugly ferocious animals, they looked like wolves with big teeth and pointy nails. Then came the giant hairy monsters with green eyes.

When they reached the Sage's monastery it was already dark. "You must be tired" stated the Sage calmly. "Let's have something to eat and then we will go to bed. Tomorrow you need to wake-up early, we have a special prayer to perform". They had some bread and soup, then they went to sleep in their separate room. There was just a mat on the floor for the Prince to sleep. He kept twisting and turning, staring at the ceiling. Unable to sleep he got up and went for a walk in the garden. He saw three sheds; he opened the first door there was lots of human skulls inside! He closed it. In the second one he found bones of limbs. He looked puzzled; he opened the third door. There was a white horse standing there laughing. "Why are you laughing?" asked the Prince.

"I am laughing at youuu" neighed the horse. "You are going to be killed tomorrow morning, the heads you saw in the shed, they are of ninety-nine brave, courageous, young men. You are going to make the hundredth. There is a statue at the back of the garden. The Sage will sacrifice you in front of his God in return he will receive a magic ring. You can wish for anything you want." Prince James closed the door and went to sleep. He knew what he had to do next.

Early morning the Sage woke the Prince up. "Go and have a bath, then we will do the prayer in the garden". After his bath the Prince came in the garden wrapped in a white cloth the Sage had left for him in the bathroom. He saw a big sharp sword leaning against the statue. There were a lamp and lots of beautiful red and yellow flowers on the ground.

"Make three rounds around the statue then kneel down". ordered the Sage. "How do I do that? I haven't done it before; can you show me please?" asked the Prince innocently.

Reluctantly the Sage went round the statue and knelt down. Without wasting any time Prince James grabbed the sword and sacrificed the Sage's life. The statue moved and a gold ring with diamond appeared. He took the ring and put it on his left hand's index finger. He changed into his princely clothes and got the horse from the shed.

They travelled through the forest for many days and nights. It was dark when they came across a pond that was glittering. The water was as red as blood. Prince James put his finger in the water, it turned gold. He dipped his sword in the pond, it turned gold. He then jumped in the pond; his clothes turned gold. He was shining so much he had to find a rag to cover his body.

"I am tired of travelling, should we have a castle here for us to live in? I have a magic ring after all" remarked the Prince to the horse. "Yeesss!" said the horse with excitement.

Prince James took his ring in his palm and said "By the power of my ring make me a castle with lots of servants". As soon as he said it a big castle appeared in front of them.

He enjoyed his freedom for a while, but then he felt bored on his own. "I need to have some friends around me, I only have a horse to talk to" he thought. The horse neighed in response. One Sunday morning he decided to go to church dressed in his gold clothes.

He saw a King and his three daughters on a chariot. He greeted them; he noticed the three princesses were very pretty especially the youngest princess. She has beautiful long blonde hair and green eyes. The princesses were very pleased to see him. Prince James rode on his horse so fast, he went to the church and came back, the King's chariot was still on its way to the church.

Back in his castle the Prince was thinking "It would be nice if I could marry one of the princesses. First, I have to find out who is worthy to be my wife." He put his rag on his shoulder to hide his identity and went to the King's palace with his horse beside him. He knocked on the door, the King's eldest daughter Sarah opened the door, one look at the Prince she pinched her nose and ran inside. The horse laughed. "Be quiet!" said the Prince. The prince knocked on the door again, another princess called Mary, slightly younger than Sarah, came and did the same as her sister. "No chance here" whispered the horse. "One last try" sighed the Prince. He knocked on the door for a third time. The youngest princess Jane opened the door. "How can I help you?" she asked.

"If the King would be so kind to grant me a piece of land to build a house that I can live in, I would be ever so grateful." he said. The Princess was very kind and sensitive. She liked to help whenever she has the opportunity, therefore, went inside and pleaded with her father to help this poor man. She came back and told the prince he can build his house in the woods far away from the palace. "Thank you" said the prince and went away.

The next day the King celebrated his birthday, he called his three daughters and asked them "By whose destiny do you live?" Princess Sarah said "I live by my fathers' destiny". Princess Mary said "I live by my fathers' destiny". "I live by my own destiny" exclaimed Princess Jane. The King was furious by Princess Jane's reply "How can she not acknowledge my power; I give her everything." he thought. The King decided to marry his eldest two daughters to Princes and married Jane to the weak smelly man in the woods. The King sent his soldiers to bring Prince James to the palace. The King married Prince James to Princess Jane without their consent. Princess Jane did not protest, she did not want to disobey her father because she loved him. The King tells Jane in her ears arrogantly "Go make your own destiny with this poor man without my money and wealth".

Jane accepted her fate and lived with her husband in the small house. Prince James told Jane "You are free to do anything you want; I am not going to force you for anything and I am going to do everything in my capacity to make your life easy."

Jane went to sleep in a separate room. She did all the chores, cooking, cleaning and washing. Her husband never gave her his clothes to wash, she found it odd but did not question him. The Prince felt sorry for Princess Jane. "I love you" he said to her. "I would do anything I could to make you happy." "I know" replied Jane in a melancholy voice.

It was a cold autumn evening, the King sent a message to Jane by a messenger, he gave her a scroll. It read "My two eldest sons-in-law are going hunting tomorrow morning, if your husband would like to join the hunts, he is most welcome." Jane hurried to her husband and informed him about the message.

"How can I go hunting, I have never hunted before".

Jane pleaded "You will have to go, everyone will laugh at me, they will say my husband is unable to do anything."

Early morning James went to his horse and said in its ear "Please do not talk in front of anyone, I do not want them to know my secret yet." Just then entered Jane. Pretending not to be able to mount his horse he complained "This horse is too big; I can't ride it." Jane tied her husband on his horse because he kept falling. She gave him a push to move forward. After a few miles, out of everyone sight the Prince took his rag off and rode his horse so fast he passed everyone else on the way to the forest.

In the forest he took his ring and said "By the power of my ring I want a castle and all the animals from the forest in my garden." everything appeared the way he wanted. The other two Princes hunted for a whole day but in vain, there were no animals to be seen. They were tired and thirsty.

At last they saw a castle, they thought they can rest for a while then carry on the hunt. On approaching the gate, they saw lots of deer and rabbits in the garden.

Prince James in his golden attire greeted them "Hello my friends, what brings you here?". The Princes told him about their predicament. "Not to worry, rest for a while then you can carry on. Prince James ordered his servants to bring some food and drinks for his guest. The two Princes were looking at each other, "Look at all those deer". said one Prince. "Let's ask the Prince for one deer to take to the palace." said the other Prince. "We can't go back empty handed." They turned to Prince James and asked him for a deer. "Yes, you can have one each, but on one condition, you let me stamp my ring on your left ankles." he said with a smile. "Of course, there is no harm in that." they both consented.

Prince James brought a rabbit home. "Make a stew and take some for your father the king. He is having a big feast I heard." Jane asked her husband to accompany her but he refused. "No, you go enjoy yourself, I need to rest." He said weakly.

The King laughed at his daughter "Look!" he said "My two sons-in-law hunted deer and your husband got a rabbit." But when the King tasted the stew he was surprised, it was so delicious and tender. The deer on the other hand was tough and chewy.

At home Prince James changed into his golden outfit and went to join his wife. He danced with her the whole night. No one knew who he was, they just wondered. Princess Jane did not show any interest in him. He returned home before his wife. On his way back he passed a beggar sleeping under a tree near his house. She woke up from the sound of the horse galloping and the bright light that was shining everywhere. She watched the Prince going in his house.

When Jane came home the old lady stopped her and told her what she saw. Jane did not believe her. In the house she found her husband asleep. "The old lady must be mistaken" she thought.

The following day war broke out. The King ordered all the men in his kingdom to go and fight.

Princess Jane again tied her husband on his horse and sent him to the battle field. Once again, the Prince rode his horse ahead of everybody else and went to the battle field. He took his ring and said "By the power of my ring I want the soldiers to surrender to me." They did and gave him the flag. On his way back he met the other two Princes and the soldiers. They were astonished and amazed. He told them he fought the battle for them, they can have the flag in return they need to give him the four corners of the flag.

That night the King had a lavish celebration, he invited all the kings and queens in the country. An invitation to Princess Jane and her husband were sent as well. As usual the prince said to Jane "You go, I am not suitable for these occasions."

Jane remembered what the old lady said before. She got dressed and said good bye to her husband. Looking around if anyone was there, she went and hid behind a tree. It was not long when her husband came out of the house in his gold garments. He mounted his horse and went to the party. Princess Jane could not believe her eyes, she was shocked. After her husband had gone, she went back in the house and searched for the old rags her husband used to wear. It was in a trunk under his bed. She took it out and hid it.

Meanwhile at the Kings' palace everyone was enjoying themselves. Prince James entered, he looked for his wife. She was nowhere to be found. Without wasting any time, he went home.

Princess Jane was waiting for him. "Who are you? Why did you hide this from me?" demanded Jane. "I have been humiliated by my family. People laughed at me when I go pass." She did not give James time to answer. "How could you do this to me? Did you enjoy making me sad?" she sobbed uncontrollably.

"I was testing you; I thought you will leave me once you found someone better than me, I want someone kind and considerate by my side that's why I went to the ball to see if you will be attracted to a richer man." confessed James.

"Does that mean you don't trust me?" inquired Jane in a furious tone.

"I do trust you and I apologise for my behaviour." replied James. Bending on one knee he said "I know you were not happy with this marriage before, I would like you to be my wife for ever, we don't have to live like this anymore. I have my own palace; we will go and live there. It is your decision, what do you say?"

"I do not care about wealth; I just want someone to love me. I stayed with you because you tried your best to make me happy." after contemplating for a moment. "Yes, I would like to be your wife forever." she said "I love you" to him for the first time and they embraced.

"Before we go, I have to tell you something." stopping the Princess from walking away. He told her about the hunting expedition and how he fought the battle. Jane was very excited. "Let's go to the palace and say good bye to my father." She got the rag and gave it to James to wear for one last time.

At last they arrived at the palace. Everyone moved aside, wondering what this poor dirty man was doing there. They were all quiet. Jane spoke "This is my husband whom my father is ashamed to call his son-in-law." She approached her father " I just wanted to let you know that the deer you so proudly announced that your eldest son-in-law hunted was given by my husband." With some arrogance in her tone she said "If you don't believe me have a look at their left ankles, you will find my husband ring stamped on them!"

The King ordered the Princes to lift up their trousers. He found the stamp.

Another thing, this party should be in my husband's honour. It was him who fought the battle and won the war. She took the four corners of the flag from her husband's pocket and showed the King.

"Bring the flag!" exclaimed the King. One soldier went and got the flag. Everyone could see the corners were missing.

Finally, she took the rag off her husband shoulders, they were all mesmerised by the shinning golden appearance.

The King felt ashamed, he said "Truly my daughter you live by your own destiny."

Among the guest Prince James parents were present. They were delighted to be reunited with their son's.

Prince James took his Princess on his horse and rode to his castle he has in the forest.

# The End.

Printed in the United States
By Bookmasters